A CARP FOR KIMIKO

by Virginia Kroll
illustrated by Katherine Roundtree

Charlesbridge

To Elena Dworkin Wright, a wonderful editor and a fabulous friend. — V.K.

Special thanks to the people who helped us learn about Japanese customs
Fumiko, Aya, and Jin Komuro,
Ayano Ninomiya,
Susan Gill of the Consulate General of Japan in Boston, and
Shiori and Keiichoro Kadoba.

Text and illustrations © 1993
by Charlesbridge Publishing

Published by
Charlesbridge Publishing
85 Main Street
Watertown, MA 02172
(617) 926-0329

Printed in Hong Kong
(LB) 10 9 8 7 6 5 4 3 2 1
(HC) 10 9 8 7 6 5 4 3 2 1

Printed on Recycled Paper.

Library of Congress Cataloging-in-Publication Data
Kroll, Virginia L.
    A carp for Kimiko / by Virginia L. Kroll; illustrated
by Katherine Roundtree.
        p.   cm.
    Summary: Although the tradition is to present
carp kites only to boys on Children's Day, Kimiko's
parents find a way to make the day special for her.
    ISBN 0-88106-413-0 (library reinforced)
    ISBN 0-88106-412-2 (trade hardcover)
    ISBN 0-88106-411-4 (softcover)
    [1. Festivals — Fiction.   2. Sex role — Fiction.   3.
Family life — Fiction.   4. Japan — Fiction.]
I. Roundtree, Katherine, ill.   II. Title.
PZ7.K9227Car   1993
[E] — dc20   93-6940
                                                     CIP
                                                     AC

Kimiko watched Papa putting up the pole. "I must fix the lowest hook this year," he said.

"For my kite?" asked Kimiko hopefully. "For baby Yukio's," Papa answered.

MAY

Kimiko ran to the calendar and counted the days. The fifth day of the fifth month would be here soon. She would ask again tomorrow.

Kimiko peeked around the door to see them. The fish kites lay flat. Kimiko knew they were saving their energy for the special day. Then they would fight the current, dancing and diving on waves of air against the blue sky and the frothy, white clouds.

Kimiko admired Taro's red and yellow fish and Tomi's blue and green fish. But it was Yukio's that made her sigh with longing. "Orange and black and white," she said, "the perfect calico carp!"

"If I had a daughter," she said, "I would let her have a fish to fly high in the blue sky, and it would be just like Yukio's." Then Kimiko pouted. "Someday I will have a daughter, but that is much too long to wait."

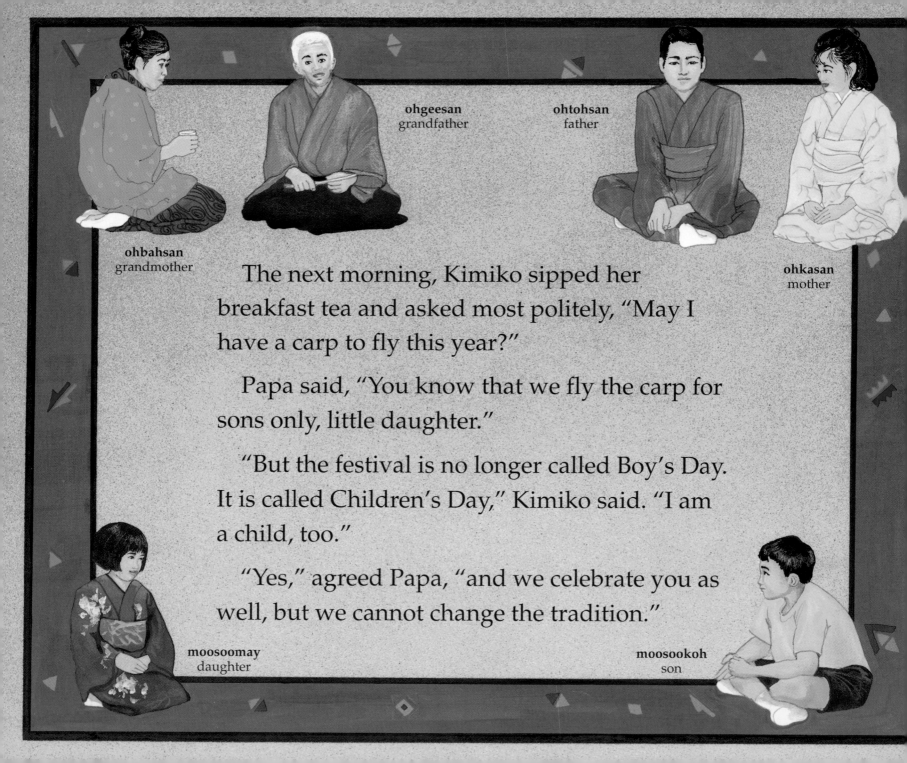

ohgeesan
grandfather

ohtohsan
father

ohbahsan
grandmother

ohkasan
mother

The next morning, Kimiko sipped her breakfast tea and asked most politely, "May I have a carp to fly this year?"

Papa said, "You know that we fly the carp for sons only, little daughter."

"But the festival is no longer called Boy's Day. It is called Children's Day," Kimiko said. "I am a child, too."

"Yes," agreed Papa, "and we celebrate you as well, but we cannot change the tradition."

moosoomay
daughter

moosookoh
son

"But I am as brave as Taro and as strong as Tomi and much, much bigger than Yukio."

"Yes," Mama repeated, "but that is the tradition."

Kimiko frowned and Mama said, "Do you remember what March 3rd was, just two months ago?"

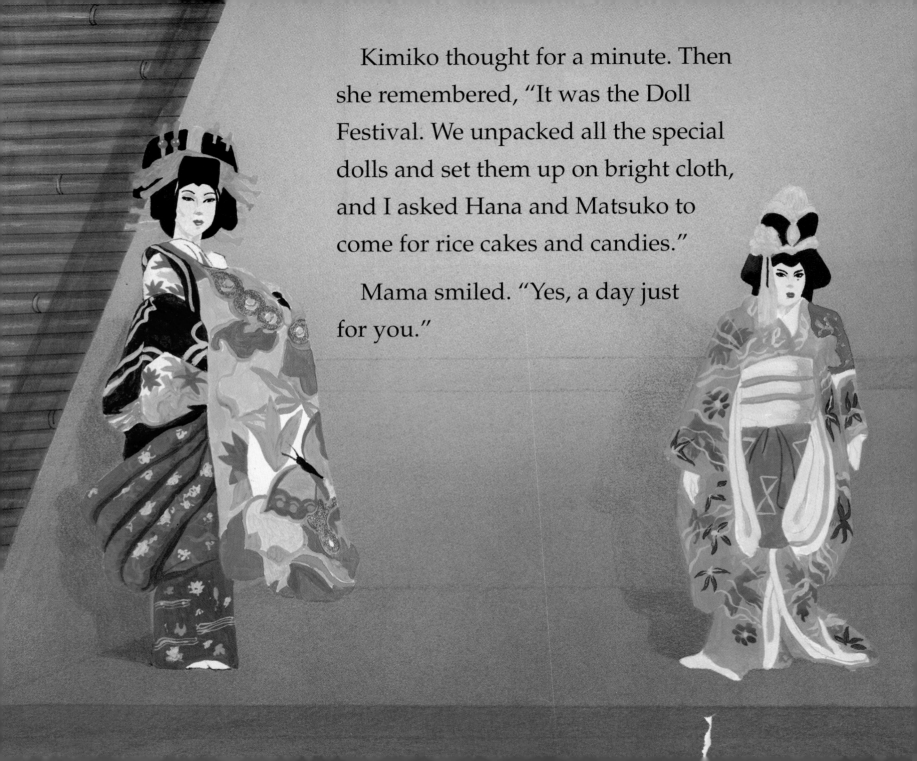

Kimiko thought for a minute. Then she remembered, "It was the Doll Festival. We unpacked all the special dolls and set them up on bright cloth, and I asked Hana and Matsuko to come for rice cakes and candies."

Mama smiled. "Yes, a day just for you."

"Not absolutely JUST for me," Kimiko recalled. "I shared it with Yukio."

"Ah yes," Mama remembered. "You let him come to your party, too."

"Even if he IS a boy," Kimiko said.

"Even if he IS a boy," Mama laughed.

"Mama?" asked Kimiko.

"Yes, little daughter?"

"Do you think we could unpack the dolls so I could see them?"

Mama shook her head. "You know the tradition, Kimiko. The dolls are not for playing. They are unpacked only once a year for their very special festival."

"But Mama, once a year is much too long to wait!" Kimiko argued.

Mama sighed. "You remind me of the carp, Kimiko, always wanting to swim against the current."

Kimiko's voice was butterfly soft. "Just one?" she dared to whisper.

Mama looked into Kimiko's eyes. "You have convinced me, little daughter."

"But," she said, holding up a firm finger, "just one."

Kimiko bowed. "Thank you, Mama."
Then she worried a bit, "Are we breaking
the tradition, Mama?"

"No, little daughter, not exactly. You might
say we are merely bending it a little."

"Like I did by sharing
my Doll Festival
Day with Yukio?"

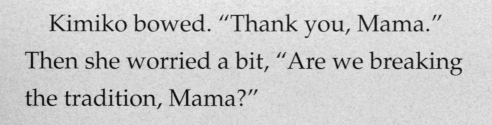

"Yes, Kimiko, like you
did by sharing your day
with Yukio," Mama said.

Children's Day dawned on Kimiko's village.

Papa hung the carp kites: one, two, three.

Kimiko held her breath. One by one they puffed to their fullest and swam, flicking their tails sideways — big, brave fish using their strength against the current. Kimiko breathed out and exclaimed, "Beautiful! Oh how I wish I had a carp!"

Tomi yelled out, "See mine? It is strongest."

Taro shouted, "Mine is fullest, see?"

Little Yukio waved his chubby hands in delight.

That night, Kimiko closed her eyes to sleep. In her dreams, the colorful carp danced wildly on the wind.

When morning came, sunshine crept under Kimiko's eyelids and pushed them awake. Kimiko blinked . . .

and blinked again. She saw a bowl of water on a tray, glistening and gleaming.

Kimiko's eyes grew wide with wonder. She peered into the cool, clear water at the beautiful fish that boldly bobbed up to the surface, all orange and black and white, the perfect calico carp.

Kimiko padded out to the table where Mama and Papa were sipping their breakfast tea. "For ME?" she asked simply.

"For you," Mama said. "A carp for Kimiko."